Book #4

THE OWLS DON'T GIVE A HOOT

Mackinac Island Press

for the love of reading

Other Buck Wilder Books

Buck Wilder's Adventures
#1 Who Stole the Animal Poop?
#2 The Work Bees Go on Strike
#3 The Ants Dig to China
#4 The Owls Don't Give a Hoot

Buck Wilder's Animal Wisdom
Buck Wilder's Small Fry Fishing Guide
Buck Wilder's Small Twig Hiking and Camping Guide
Buck Wilder's Little Skipper Boating Guide

...and more to come...

#5 The Salmon Stop Running
#6 The Squirrels Go Nuts

Buck Wilder's Animal Adventures #4: The Owls Don't Give A Hoot
Written by Timothy R. Smith

Copyright 2007 Timothy R. Smith

First Edition
Library of Congress Cataloging-in-Publication Data

Smith, Timothy R.

Buck Wilder's Adventures #4
The Owls Don't Give A Hoot

Summary: Buck Wilder and friends work to solve why the owls no longer give
a hoot and stop being the time keepers of the woods.

ISBN13 978-1-934133-11-8

Fiction
10 9 8 7 6 5 4 3 2 1

A Mackinac Island Press, Inc. publication
Traverse City, Michigan

www.mackinacislandpress.com

Printed in the United States

Buck Wilder

"Be nice to nature and
nature will be nice to you"

B.W.

THE OWLS DON'T
GIVE A HOOT

CHAPTERS

INTRODUCTION

Buck Wilder's earlier adventure stories (books one, two, and three) have a much longer introduction and a greater description of who Buck Wilder is, where he lives, and who his animal friends are. This is just a shorter introduction in case you haven't read them.

First, Buck Wilder lives in a house that is way back in the woods, over the stream, beyond the pond, and where all the animal trails go. It is a huge awesome looking house that is built up in the trees. It is a tree house like something you have never seen before. It looks kind of like this:

In this tree house lives Buck Wilder. He is a very nice and friendly man who loves nature, understands a lot about the woods and is friends with all the animals that are around him. You can always count on Buck Wilder to have some extra food or be of help, if needed.

Buck Wilder looks kind of like this:

Buck Wilder has a whole bunch of animal friends. They often come to visit to see what he is cooking, talk a little about life in the woods, or to see what Buck's new book is about. Buck loves to write stories about what he learns from nature and the many adventures that happen in the woods. Of all his animal friends he has one favorite, Rascal Raccoon. Most of the time Rascal lives in the tree house with Buck, doing a few household chores and helping out with some detective work, when needed. Buck and Rascal are good friends.

Rascal Raccoon looks kind of like this:

So, give the page a flip and let's get on with the story!

CHAPTER 1

IT ALL STARTED LIKE THIS

One day in the woods, late in the morning, while Buck, Rascal, and the fish in the aquarium were all sleeping in late, the bell rang. And, as you know, when the bell rings there is a visitor that has come to Buck's house.

Not realizing what time it was Rascal hollered, "Hello down there. Who comes to visit us so early in the day?"

"It is me, Herman Turkey. I've come to see Buck and it is not so early in the day!"

Sure enough, as soon as Rascal fully woke up to his morning senses, he looked out the window and saw the sun was already way up. He realized that both he and Buck had once again overslept by a lot.

Hearing the commotion Buck sat up in bed, rubbed the sleep from his eyes, gave a morning stretch and said, "Hey Rascal, what is going on? Have we overslept again? This is the fourth morning in a row. What is going on with our alarm clock?"

"That is a good question, Buck. Let's ask our alarm clock. I'll get the ladder down right now and we can ask

Just then Herman Turkey hollered up, "Hey Rascal, you don't need to lower the ladder. I can just fly up. It is a lot easier." So with a few beats of his big feathered wings, Herman Turkey flew up to Buck's tree house.

"Good morning everyone," said Herman.

"A very good morning to you," replied Buck and Rascal.

"Wow," said Buck. "It is getting late in the morning. I better get some breakfast going. How about some oatmeal and raisins? Maybe with a little toasted cornbread?"

"Sounds delicious, Buck," replied Herman. Turkeys love to eat anything with corn in it.

"As I get myself going," said Buck, "Herman, would you please tell me why you, my morning alarm clock, did not get us up this morning?"

21

CHAPTER 2

THE ALARM SYSTEM

To better understand the question that Buck is asking, you need to understand the alarm system that works in the woods. There are all types of alarm systems in the woods. There is the warning alarm system that animals use to warn others of a problem in the woods. If there is a potential danger, the squirrels will chatter from the tree tops, the crows will yell in the air, the deer will grunt, and the robins will screech. There is a food alarm, there is a stranger-in-the-woods alarm, there is a storm-coming alarm, and there is a wake-up-in-the-morning alarm.

You also need to know that not everything in the woods wakes up at the same time. There is an order to the wake-up system. The owls wake up the crows, the crows wake up the robins, the robins wake up the turkeys, etc, until everyone in the woods is up and moving.

It all starts with the owl. The owl is the timekeeper of the woods. Owls love to sit up in the tallest trees they can find and call out the time throughout the night. They will rotate their heads so that everyone can hear and they will make a call across the woods, "Hoot, time for bed. Hoot, it's late!" Then every hour on the hour, "Hoot, should be one…Hoot, should be two…" Right up to daybreak.

Hi, I'm Virgil the Owl and my job is to give a hoot!

That is when they will make their final calls of the day, "Hoot, time is it. Hoot, time to get up." Then the crows take over with their early morning "Caw-Caws." They will yell back at the owl, "Caws you are up, caws I'm up. Caw-caw, call everyone, call everyone." They wake up the rest of the birds. The robins start to sing and then the wild turkeys join in with a roaring "Buck, Buck, Buck." Real soon all the birds are chattering back and forth which wakes up the rest of the animals in the woods. It is a very simple wake up system and it has been going on forever.

Well, Buck's alarm clock is a flock of wild turkeys that lives next to his tree house and sleeps in his trees during the night. Every morning when they wake up, as they fly down to the ground, they love to call out Buck's name and wake him up. "Buck, Buck, Buck. Wake up, Buck. Time for coffee, Buck. Buck, Buck, Buck." It is a very natural alarm clock and he likes it a lot.

The problem is Buck has been oversleeping and he wants to ask Herman Turkey what is going on.

CHAPTER 3

WHAT IS GOING ON, HERMAN?

"Buck, I am sleeping in too," Herman Turkey replied to Buck's question. "All the turkeys are. The crows haven't been waking us up and I don't know why. The rhythm of the woods is off and everybody is sleeping in."

"Oh!" said Buck, continuing to rub

his wake up eyes. "That is a problem. If the animals are not getting up at their proper times and everyone is sleeping in like us, then the cycle of life in the woods is off. The early bird is not catching the early worm. The roosters are not 'cock-a-doodling' to the morning sunrise and the ducks aren't 'quacking.' I wonder what is going on."

"Rascal," Buck continued. "Since you are the best detective in the woods, and have such a good relationship with all the other animals, would you please do me a favor? Go with Herman Turkey, ask your animal friends what is going on, and see if you can find out why everyone is sleeping in."

"Oh," said Rascal, "I love it when there is a problem or dilemma and I can help figure it out. Come on, Herman. Let's go see what we can find out." And off they went.

As they went down the trail that led from Buck's house, the one that went through the big tall pine trees and along the edge of Buck's favorite fishing stream, Herman said to Rascal, "Let's go visit the crows and ask them why they are not waking us up in the morning. That is their morning wake up job and they are not doing it."

"Good idea," said Rascal. "I should have thought of that!"

CHAPTER 4

WHAT'S UP, CRAINIUM?

Herman and Rascal took off to where the crows spent their days near the edge of the woods. Crows like to fly out from the edge of the woods, look for corn, berries, or small food in nearby fields and then fly back to the tallest trees and tell everyone what they just ate. They will holler out things like, "Caw, Caw, caws I'm full. Caws, that was good. Caws, I ate all I can eat." Crows are big black birds. They are very smart and like to fly in big groups. They are a little selfish, don't get along with other big birds like owls and eagles, and they sometimes like to show off to their friends.

Hi, I'm Crainium Crow because I have a big head... in many ways!

Upon arriving at the edge of the woods the first crow that Rascal and Herman met was Crainium Crow. Crainium was one of the elder crows. The other crows respected him. When he spoke he wasted few words and got right to the point.

"How goes it?" asked Rascal.

"Better than the average bird," replied Crainium. Before Rascal and Herman had a chance to say anything else Crainium continued, "I bet you are here to find out why we haven't been waking you up in the morning, right?"

"That is right," replied Rascal. "What is going on with our morning alarm system?"

"I wish I knew," replied Crainium.

Looking at Herman Turkey, Crainium continued, "We haven't been waking you up because the owls haven't been waking us up and we have been sleeping in too. The whole rhythm of our day is off. I would like to ask the owls what the problem is, but as everyone knows we crows don't get along very well with the owls. We rarely come to agreement on anything and usually just end up yelling at each other. Do you think you could talk to the owls for us?"

"Glad to," replied Rascal. "We would like to find out what is going on."

"This is real detective work," Rascal said to Herman. "It is fun trying to solve a problem or figure out a dilemma. I love being a raccoon because solving problems is one of the things we do best. Let's go find Virgil the Owl and ask him what is going on." So off went Rascal and Herman Turkey once again to solve the mystery of the missing wake-up calls.

CHAPTER 5

ASK THE OWLS

To find owls during the day, is normally not an easy task, because owls like to stay up all night and sleep all day. When they sleep, they sleep real soundly and don't like to be awakened unless it is an emergency. They will find a nice soft corner of a tree or will snuggle into an old hole in a trunk for a long day's sleep.

Herman and Rascal headed for the thick part of the woods, the place where the evergreens grew tall and close together. The wind had a hard time getting into this part of the woods. It is a very quiet place and a great place to take a daytime sleep.

As Herman and Rascal entered the thick, dark part of the forest they looked at each other and Rascal said, "Shhhhh…walk softly and try not to make too much noise. We don't want to wake up all the owls. We'll just wake up the first one we find." To their surprise that did not happen. As they entered the thick part of the woods they heard a group of owls talking to each other. The owls were awake and just conversing back and forth:

> "Hoot-this and Hoot-that."
> "Hoot made that decision?"
> "Hoot do you think you are?"

They were sitting upright on tree
limbs in almost a perfect circle in the
middle of the woods.

As Rascal and Herman came near the circle, the owls began to get quiet and said, "Hoot goes there? Hoot is coming? Hoot do you want?"

Rascal and Herman stopped a distance away and said, "Hello there. This is Rascal Raccoon and Herman Turkey. Do you mind if we enter?"

"Come on in. You are always welcome," was the reply. As Herman and Rascal entered the circle of owls. Rascal spotted the biggest and the oldest of them all, Virgil the Owl, who was sitting on the highest part of the branch.

"How is my good friend Virgil?" said Rascal, with Herman standing by his side.

"Hoot hello," responded Virgil. Because he was the oldest he spoke on behalf of all the owls. "What brings my friend Rascal Raccoon and Herman

Turkey to our part of the woods, and in the middle of the day?"

"We have a problem," said Rascal. "Everyone in the woods is sleeping in. The turkeys aren't waking up Buck. The crows aren't waking up the turkeys and from what we understand, you owls are not waking up the crows. There is no morning wake up call. What is going on? Can you owls please explain?"

CHAPTER 6

WE TAKE GREAT PRIDE IN OUR WORK

"I would be glad to explain," replied Virgil. "We don't give a hoot anymore. There will be no more hoots from us. We are finished! Done! We don't give a hoot anymore!"

Rascal and Herman looked at the owls in almost disbelief of what they had just heard. "Animals don't quit. Ever. What is this all about?" asked

Rascal. "Would you please explain?"

"Okay," responded Virgil. "We owls take great pride in our work. We are the timekeepers of the woods and we are very proud of it. Every night, just before dark, when the color of day goes away and the black and white of night starts to appear, we fly up into the tallest tree we can find, perch ourselves

on the very top and begin calling out the time of the night, all night long. We rotate our heads and make calls in every direction just so all the animals will hear us. It is very important that all can hear throughout the night. Right up to the early morning sunrise."

"I agree," said Rascal. "So what is the problem?"

"The problem," responded Virgil, "is that our biggest and tallest trees, the ones we like to perch on the very top of, are disappearing. First, we thought they were dying of old age and just falling down, but we just found out that someone is cutting them down. We can't make our calls from small trees in the woods—no one would hear us. We have to be way up on top. With the big tall trees gone, we can't give a hoot anymore!"

"Ohhh, this is not good," responded Rascal. "We need you owls up there every night, because if you are not, everything in the woods is off. When we lose our wake up system the timing of our day is off. We better go tell Buck what we have found out. He will know what to do." So off went Rascal and Herman heading back to the tree house.

CHAPTER 7

BACK TO THE TREE HOUSE

As they came close to the tree house they could smell that Buck was cooking up something good. As soon as they entered the tree house Buck said, "Welcome back. You both left in such a hurry this morning that I never got a chance to make you a morning breakfast. Before you start to tell me what you found out, come on in here, get a seat at the table, and let's eat a late morning meal." Knowing how much wild turkeys love to eat corn, Buck made Herman a batch of hot corn muffins with a little honey on the side. For Buck and Rascal there were fresh blueberries, raspberries, a bowl of cereal, and hot chocolate. Yum!!

They all started to eat. "Well, Mr. Detective," asked Buck while looking at Rascal, "what did you find out?"

"Lots," replied Rascal, and he explained what he saw and learned from his morning adventure.

"Hmmmmm," said Buck as he heard about the crows. "Ohhhh," he said learning about the owls and then, "oh no," he said when he heard about big trees going missing. "As soon as we are done eating and cleaning the dishes, I think I will put on my hiking boots and go for a walk in the woods. I need to see what is going on."

"I'll stay and clean up," said Herman. "Great meal, Buck. Thanks a lot!"

51

So, after Buck put on his hiking boots, he and Rascal headed out into the woods. The first thing Buck noticed was that many of the trees in the woods had decorative ribbons wrapped around them. Some were yellow, some were blue, and some were red. "I wonder what this is all about," said Buck.

"I saw these ribbons before," responded Rascal. "I think someone is decorating for a party. Why else would you put ribbons in the woods? It looks like it is going to be a big party because there are ribbons everywhere."

"Hmmmm," said Buck as he scratched his head. This meant he was trying to figure something out.

CHAPTER 8

THE SOUND OF SAWS

As Buck and Rascal continued their walk through the woods off in the distance they began to hear the screech and roar of what sounded like big trucks and machinery. As they came closer they could clearly hear the sounds of tractor wheels, chain saws running, and men hollering at each other. They sounded like they were looking for Tim.

They were hollering, "Hey
Tim, Tim, Timber," and then
came a loud crash. It didn't
take long before Buck realized
all the noise was coming from a
tree-cutting crew. It was a group of
men wearing hard hats, glasses, big

gloves, and cutting down
trees with chain saws.

"Wow," said Buck. "We
should go over, say hello, and
find out what this is all about."
So they did.

As soon as Buck came into view

the men immediately stopped cutting trees, put down their saws, put big smiles on their faces, and waved a friendly "hello." They all knew who Buck Wilder was and they respected him for his knowledge of the woods and how friendly he was with the animals. "Hey everyone, Buck Wilder is here."

"Hi, Buck!"

"Catching any big fish, Buck?" came the friendly welcomes from the men.

"I have been catching some real nice fish lately. I found a fishing spot where the fish are so friendly that they will just jump right into your pocket and you don't even need to use a fishing pole!" said Buck, chuckling.

All the men laughed a little and said, Oh, sure Buck. You tell the best fishing stories."

"I'm not kidding," said Buck. "Come on with me and I'll show you the spot."

Big Mike, who was the boss of the work crew, looked over with a big smile and said, "It is time we all took a break. Let's go fishing with Buck."

All the men said in unison, "Yeah, we get to go fishing with Buck Wilder. Yeah!"

Buck knew that most people liked to go fishing and it was always relaxing and a good time to talk among friends.

So off they went into the woods with Buck Wilder leading, the men following, and Rascal trailing from behind. Rascal, like most of the animals in the woods, was a little fearful of strangers, especially people strangers. The animals never knew who was friendly or who was a hunter or trapper, so they learned to just keep their distance.

CHAPTER 9

WHAT IS GOING ON?

On the way through the woods Buck asked Big Mike "What is going on? Why are you and the others cutting down trees in the woods?"

"Because we need the wood," replied Big Mike. "There are houses to be built, buildings to put up, and furniture to be made. There are a lot of people out there that need a roof over their head. This forest has a lot of trees in it and there is a lot of wood that people could use for building. Just look at this big beauty right here," said Big Mike, pointing to a tall white pine tree with a red ribbon wrapped around it.

This tree is a beauty!

"We marked this one as one we can't miss. The blue ribbons mark the trees that are our second choice and the yellows are just maybes."

"Okay," said Buck, "that explains why so many ribbons are in the woods."

"Kind of looks like a big birthday party, doesn't it, Buck?" said Big Mike with a laugh. Buck wasn't laughing.

It wasn't long before they arrived at one of Buck's favorite fishing spots. It was next to a beautiful little stream with crystal clear water and packed full of happy smiling fish. They were always happy and smiling, because most of the time when Buck caught them, he would release them so that he could catch them again on another day. It was kind of like a game and the fish knew it. It was fun and it kept the fish smiling and happy.

As soon as Buck reached the edge of the stream a couple of the fish jumped up out of the water and had big smiles on their faces.

"Watch this," said Buck, as he stepped into the water. He opened his pocket and a fish jumped right out of the water into his pocket...and it was smiling too!

CHAPTER 10

BE GOOD TO NATURE

"Did you see that?" said one of the men.

"I can't believe my eyes," said another.

"Unbelievable," said another.

Big Mike stepped up. "I have never seen anything like that in my life," he said. "Buck, how did you do that?"

"It's real simple," replied Buck.

"I have learned that if you are good to nature then nature will be good to you. These fish have learned that I am just here to have fun. Sometimes they come up with a smile. Sometimes they will pull real hard on my fishing line. Sometimes they will even break my line and jump out of the water and laugh while they swim away. They make it fun," said Buck as he took the fish from his pocket and slid it back in the water.

"Big fish, you come back another day," said Buck as the fish swam away.

"Buck, you are awesome," said Big Mike. "I could learn a lot from you."

"Oh, it's easy," replied Buck. "All you have to do is be fair and do what is right. Just like the trees you are cutting down. I know that people need wood for all kinds of building projects. My own house is built mostly out of wood. But when I cut the trees to build it, I tried to use trees of all sizes and not just from one area of the woods. I picked them from different parts of the woods so that you didn't even know any were missing. You see, the animals in the woods also need those trees for their homes and shelters. They raise their families in, under, and around those trees. Those trees offer protection, safety, and sometimes even food to many animals. The very short ones are needed and the very tall ones serve a purpose, too. You need to selectively cut trees in the woods…and for every tree you cut, you should plant two. It is giving back to nature, and before you know it, the fish will be jumping in your pocket."

"Like I said before Buck, you are awesome," said Big Mike. "Every time I run into you I learn something new. No wonder all the animals like you so much."

All of the men standing around and listening nodded their heads in agreement and said, "Thanks, Buck! We needed to hear that, too!"

"Come on," said Big Mike to the others. "Let's get back, remove a bunch of those ribbons and start planting some trees…and then let's go fishing!"

"Yeah!" responded everyone and off they went.

"See you later, Buck," said Big Mike.

"Next time bring a fishing pole," said Buck. "Just in case!"

They all laughed as they headed back down the trail.

CHAPTER 11

BUCK DID THE JOB

Up stepped Rascal saying, "Buck, I think you did the job. Not only did you stop those men from cutting down all the trees, you got them to save most of the big ones and the small ones... and they are going to plant a bunch of new trees! Wait until I tell the rest of the animals in the woods, especially the owls. Now they can fly up to the tall trees and start keeping time again in the woods. I sure miss hoot calls in the woods. Maybe everything will get back to normal again and there will be no more sleeping in. I am out of here," said Rascal and off he went in a hurry.

Buck turned to go back to his tree house. As he turned he gave a wink toward the stream and said, "Thanks for the help." Just then a big fish jumped from the water, wiggled a little, gave a wave with his tail, and said, "No problem, Buck. Come back another day. That was fun!"

Off went Buck just whistling a tune, happy that he could help.

During the next few days the timber men moved through the woods and selectively cut only a few trees here and there. They tried to leave as many tall ones as possible and planted two trees for every one they cut down. The animals stayed out of their way and hid until they were gone.

It didn't take long for the owls to learn that their tallest and favorite watchtower trees were saved and that they could get back to being the timekeepers of the woods. Virgil the Owl put a big smile back on his round face, flew up to the top of the tallest tree he could find and let out a boisterous call, "Hoot I'm back. Hoot, did you miss me? Now I can give a HOOT! Hoot! HOOT!"

CHAPTER 12

BACK TO NORMAL

Soon things were back to normal. The crows woke up on time, the turkeys called out "Buck," the roosters crowed, and the early birds caught the worms. Life was back on schedule—a natural schedule.

Buck and Rascal went back to their normal life in the tree house. Rascal played the catch and release game with the fish in the aquarium, took long naps, and helped Buck with the household chores. Buck cooked a lot for his animal friends, wrote stories about his adventures in the woods, and went fishing as often as he could.

Everything was good for a long time until one day Rascal discovered a real problem in the woods and all the animals needed Buck's help. It was the time when the salmon stopped running and Mother Nature didn't like it! You can read about it in Buck Wilder's next outdoor adventure story, 'The Time the Salmon Stopped Running!' Until then, have fun outdoors and remember: be nice to nature and nature will be nice to you!

SECRET MESSAGE DECODING PAGE

Hidden in this book is a secret Buck Wilder message. You need to figure it out. Hidden in many of the drawings are letters that, when put together, make up a statement, a Buck Wilder statement. Your job is to find those letters and always remember the message – it's important.

DO NOT write in this book if it's from the library, your classroom, or borrowed from someone.

If you need help finding the hidden letters turn the page.

16 letters make up 4 words.

The secret letters are hidden on the following pages in this order…

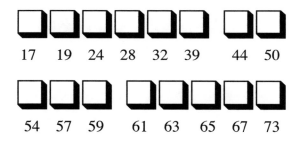

| 17 | 19 | 24 | 28 | 32 | 39 | | 44 | 50 |

| 54 | 57 | 59 | | 61 | 63 | 65 | 67 | 73 |

16 letters make up 4 words.

Remember – Don't Write in this Book!

Mackinac Island Press

for the love of reading